For Oscar, Ralph and Paul with love,
and with special thanks to the man in the Land Rover.

First American edition 2005
by Kane/Miller Book Publishers, Inc.
La Jolla, California

On the Road copyright @ Frances Lincoln Limited 2005
Text and illustrations copyright © Susan Steggall 2005
On the Road was edited, designed and produced by Frances Lincoln Limited,
4 Torriano Mews, Torriano Avenue, London NW5 2RZ

Library of Congress Control Number: 2004109116

Printed and Bound in China

1 2 3 4 5 6 7 8 9 10

ISBN 1-929132-70-0

ON THE ROAD

Susan Steggall

Kane/Miller
BOOK PUBLISHERS

Off we go

along the road

past the garage

up the hill

around the corner

through the roadworks

STOP!

Down the hill

into the tunnel

across the junction

under the bridge

over the fields

to the sea!